This book belongs to

_____

_____

Aged _____

THE
Singing Bear

AND OTHER STORIES

THE
Singing Bear
AND OTHER STORIES

p

This is a Parragon Book
This edition published in 2002

Parragon
Queen Street House
4 Queen Street
Bath BA1 1HE, UK

Copyright © Parragon 2000

ISBN 0-75258-419-7

Designed by Mik Martin

Printed in Italy

These stories have been previously
published by Parragon in the
Bumper Bedtime Series

CONTENTS

The Singing Bear

LONG AGO, there lived a young boy named Peter. He was a gentle lad who loved all creatures, but most of all he loved the animals and birds of the forest. Many a time he had mended a jay's broken wing, or set a badger free from a cruel trap.

One day, the fair came to town and Peter was very excited. He could see brightly coloured tents being put up in the field and carts arriving with mysterious looking loads. As soon as the fair was open Peter was off with his penny in his pocket to try his luck. First of all he had a go at the coconut shy. Then he tried to climb the greasy pole.

Finally, he used his last farthing on the tombola stall. He was about to head for home when out of the corner of his eye he caught a glimpse of a dreadful sight. Lying in a cage, looking sad and forlorn, was a large brown bear. On a small plate at the front of the cage was the bear's name: Lombard. He looked so dejected that Peter immediately vowed to set him free. The cage was strongly padlocked and Peter knew not how he could break the lock. He turned to make his way home, with the bear gazing pitifully after him.

That night, Peter tossed and turned in his bed. What was he to do? He wasn't strong enough to break into the bear's cage and his keeper would surely not agree to set him free. In the middle of the night, he resolved to return to the fairground to comfort the bear.

He slipped out of bed and made his way by the light of the moon back to the fairground. To his astonishment he found the bear singing a song to himself in a beautiful voice. For a while Peter listened to the lovely sound of the bear's singing. Then he had an idea. He remembered a piece of paper he had seen pinned to the palace gate.

"Don't cry, Lombard," he said.

"I think I know a way to get you out of here. But first you must teach me your song." The bear was happy to oblige and soon the two of them were singing the song together. Then Peter said, "I must go, but I'll be back tomorrow. And remember, when you see me, be ready to sing your song."

The next day, Peter put on his very best clothes and set off for the palace. Pinned to the gate was the piece of paper, just as Peter had remembered. On the paper was written in a handsome script:

The King Requires a Minstrel with a Fine Voice. Apply Within.

Peter knocked at the gate. He

was shown into a beautiful golden gallery where a row of minstrels were waiting to be auditioned. A courtier rang a little bell for silence, and in came the king. He sat down at his great gold throne.

"Let the audition begin," cried the king. The first minstrel stepped forward. He sang a song in a sweet, high voice that tugged at the heart and reduced the court to tears. The next minstrel sang in a deep, rich voice that sent shivers down the spine, so that the birds in the trees stopped singing to listen. The next minstrel sang a song that was so witty and amusing that the entire court wept with laughter.

At last it was Peter's turn. He stepped forward, gave a deep bow and said, "I beg your majesty's permission to perform my song out of doors, so that all the wild creatures of the forest might hear it, too."

"What a strange request!" said the king. However, if the truth be told, he had grown quite sleepy listening to so many beautiful songs and thought the fresh air might liven him up. "Very well, but it had better be worth it!" he said, giving Peter a fierce look.

"Follow me!" called Peter. He led the king, the court and all the

minstrels out of the palace gates
and down the road.

"Where are we going?" and
"This is very untoward," they
muttered.

At last they reached the fairground, but Peter didn't stop until
he was in view of Lombard's cage.
Lombard saw him and Peter winked
at the bear.

"This is where I'd like to sing
for you," said Peter to the king.

The king's royal eyebrows rose
higher and higher as he looked
around him. "Well, I must say this is
very odd indeed! However, as we've
come this far, we may as well hear
your song. Proceed!" said the king.

Peter opened his mouth and mimed the words while Lombard sang. It was the most beautiful song that anyone had ever heard. By the end of the song, the king was sobbing tears of joy, mirth and sorrow all together.

"That was the finest song I ever heard," he said. "You have won the audition and I would like you to be my minstrel."

Peter took another low bow. "Sire," he said. "Would that I could accept, but in all honesty it was not I who sang but my friend, Lombard the bear."

Everyone gasped as they saw the bear in his cage.

For a moment the king looked furious. But then he began to smile and said, "I praise you for your honesty, Peter, and I would very much like to have Lombard for my minstrel. Chancellor, bring me the royal purse."

The king paid Lombard's keeper handsomely, who was then delighted to set the bear free. Lombard became the king's minstrel and was famous throughout the land, and from then on Peter went to the palace each day and sang duets with his friend, the bear. And it is said that, in the end, Peter married the king's daughter.

Mrs Mouse's Holiday

RS MOUSE was very excited. All year she had been *so* busy. First there had been nuts and berries to gather in readiness for winter. Then she had needed to give her little house a big spring clean to make it nice and fresh. Now, as the warm sun shone down on the trees and flowers of her woodland home, she had promised herself a well-deserved holiday. But getting ready for holidays seemed to make one busier than ever! There was so much to do!

First she took out her little case, opened it and placed it carefully on her neatly made bed.

Then she rushed to her cupboard
and selected some fine holiday
dresses. Back to her case she
scuttled and laid them in. Now she
chose several pairs of shoes — a
nice pair of sandals for walking
along the front in, a pair of smart
shoes for shopping in, an even
smarter pair for going to dinner in,
and another pair just in case!

"I'll need a couple of sun hats,"
she thought to herself, and so into
the case they went as well. These

were followed by a coat, some gloves and a scarf (just in case the breeze got up and it became cold). Then, in case it became very sunny, in went some sunglasses, some sun cream and a sunshade. But, oh dear, there were so many things in the case that it refused to shut. She tried sitting on it, and bouncing on it, but still it stubbornly would not close.

So out from the case came all the things that she had just put in, and Mrs Mouse scurried to the cupboard again and chose an even bigger case. This time they all fitted perfectly, and she shut the case with a big sigh of relief.

Now she was ready to go to the seaside for her holiday. She sat on the train, with her case on the rack above her head, munching her hazel nut sandwiches and looking eagerly out of the window hoping to see the sea. Finally, as the train chuffed around a bend, there it was! A great, deep blue sea shimmering in the sun, with white gulls soaring over the cliffs and headlands.

"I'm really looking forward to a nice, quiet rest," she said to herself.

Her guest house was very comfortable, and so close to the sea that she could smell the clean, salty air whenever she opened her window. "This is the life," she thought. "Nice and peaceful."

After she had put her clothes away, she put on her little swimming costume and her sun hat and packed her beach bag. Now she was ready for some peaceful sunbathing!

At the beach, she found herself a quiet spot, closed her eyes and was soon fast asleep. But not for long! A family of voles had arrived on the beach, and they weren't trying to have a quiet time at all. The youngsters in the family yelled at the top of their voices, splashed water everywhere, and sent their beach ball tumbling all over Mrs

Mouse's neatly laid out beach towel.

Just as Mrs Mouse thought that it couldn't get any noisier, along came a crowd of ferrets. Now if you've ever sat on a beach next to a crowd of ferrets, you'll know what it's like. Their noisy shouting and singing made Mrs Mouse's head buzz.

Mrs Mouse couldn't stand it a moment longer. She was just wondering where she might find some peace and quiet when she spotted a rock just a little way out to sea.

"If I swim out to that rock," she thought, "I will surely have some peace and quiet there." So she gathered up her belongings and swam over to the rock. It was a bit lumpy, but at least it was quiet. Soon she was fast asleep again.

Just then the rock started to move slowly out to sea! It wasn't really a rock at all, you see, but a turtle which had been dozing near the surface. Off into the sunset it went, with Mrs Mouse dozing on its back, quite unaware of what was happening.

Eventually, the turtle came to a deserted island. At that moment, Mrs Mouse woke up. She looked at the empty beach, and without even knowing she had been sleeping on a turtle, she jumped off and swam to the shore, thinking it was the beach that she had just left.

Just then, the turtle swam off, and Mrs Mouse suddenly realised what had happened. For a moment she was horrified. But then she looked at the quiet, palm-fringed beach with no-one about but herself, and thought of the noisy beach she had just left.

"Well, perhaps this isn't such a

bad place to spend a quiet holiday after all," she thought.

And that's just what she did. Day after day she lazed on her own private beach with no-one to disturb her. There were plenty of coconuts and fruits to eat, and she wanted for nothing. She even made herself a cozy bed from palm leaves.

Eventually, though, she started to miss her own little house in the woods and decided it was time to get back home. First she took half a coconut and nibbled out the tasty inside. "That will make a fine boat to sit in," she said.

Next she found a palm leaf and

stuck it in the bottom of the shell. She took her little boat to the water's edge and, as the wind caught her palm leaf sail, off she floated back to the boarding house to get her belongings.

As she sailed back she thought, "This is the quietest holiday I've ever had. I may come back here next year!"

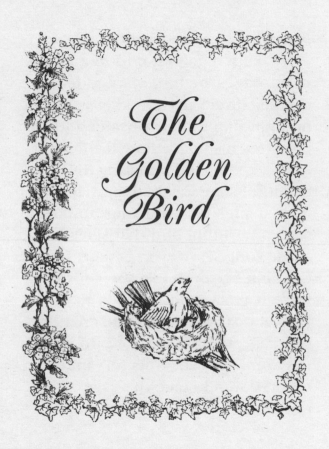

The Golden Bird

THERE WAS ONCE a king who kept a golden bird in a gilded cage. The bird wanted for nothing. Every day the king's servant brought him food and water and groomed his fine yellow feathers. And each day the bird sang his beautiful song for the king. "How lucky I am," cried the king, "to have such a beautiful bird that sings such a fine song." However, as time passed the king began to feel sorry for the bird. "It really isn't fair," he thought, "to keep such a handsome creature in a cage. I must give the bird its freedom." He called his servant and ordered him to take the cage into the jungle and release the bird.

The servant obeyed, and took the cage deep into the jungle where he came to a small clearing. He set the cage down, opened the door and out hopped the golden bird. "I hope you can look after yourself," the servant said as he walked away.

The golden bird looked about him. "This is strange!" he thought to himself. "Still, I suppose someone will come along to feed me soon." He settled down and waited.

After a while he heard a crashing sound in the trees, and then he saw a monkey swinging from branch to branch on his long arms.

"Hello there!" called the

monkey, hanging by his tail and casting the bird an upside down grin. "Who are you?"

"I am the golden bird," replied the golden bird haughtily.

"I can see you're new around here," said the monkey. "I'll show you the best places to feed in the tree tops."

"No thanks," replied the golden bird ungratefully. "What could an ape like you possibly teach me? You've got such a funny face. I expect you're envious of my beautiful beak," he added.

"Have it your own way," called the monkey as he swung off into the trees.

Some time later the golden bird heard a hissing noise in the undergrowth and a snake came slithering by.

"Well, hello," hissed the snake. "Who are you?"

"I am the golden bird," replied the golden bird proudly.

"Let me show you the jungle paths," said the snake.

"No thanks," replied the bird rudely. "What could a snake possibly teach me? With your horrid hissing voice, you must be jealous of my beautiful song," he said, forgetting that he had not opened his beak to sing yet.

"Very well," hissed the snake as

he slithered away into the under-growth.

By now the golden bird was beginning to wonder when his food would arrive. He began to imagine the tasty morsel that he hoped he would soon be eating. Just then he was aware of a movement on the tree trunk behind him. Looking up he caught a glimpse of a chameleon, lying camouflaged against the trunk.

"Good day," said the chameleon. "I've been here all the time, so I know who you are. You're the golden bird. I've heard you say it twice. It's a good idea to know where to hide in case of danger. Let me show you."

"No thanks," replied the golden bird. "What could an ugly brute like you possibly teach me? You must wish you had lovely feathers like me," he said, fluffing up his beautiful, golden plumage.

"Don't say I didn't warn you," muttered the chameleon as he darted away.

The golden bird had just settled down again when a great grey shadow passed over the jungle. He looked up to see an eagle swooping low over the trees. The monkey swung up to hide in the densest foliage near the top of the trees. The snake slid into the deepest part of the undergrowth.

The chameleon stayed quite still but his skin colour became a perfect match for the tree he was on and he became totally invisible.

"Aha!" thought the golden bird. "All I have to do is fly away and that stupid eagle will never catch up with me." He flapped his wings

and flapped and flapped, but he did not know that his wings had grown weak through living a life of luxury in the palace. Now the bird regretted his golden plumage and wished that he had dull brown feathers that would not show up in

the forest clearing. For his fine yellow feathers made him easy to see. He was sure the eagle would come and gobble him up. "Help!" he trilled. "Please help me someone." Now he could see the eagle swooping down towards him with eyes blazing like fire and talons drawn.

At that moment the golden bird felt something close around his legs and pull him into the undergrowth. It was the snake. Then he was lifted up into the trees by a long, hairy arm and saw he was being carried by the monkey.

"Keep still," whispered the chameleon pushing him into the

centre of a large yellow flower. "The eagle won't see you there." And sure enough, the golden bird found that he was precisely the colour of the flower and the eagle flew straight past him.

"However can I repay you all?" exclaimed the bird. "You saved my life!"

"You can sing for us," replied the animals. And from then on, the monkey, the snake and the chameleon looked after the golden bird, and he sang his beautiful song for them every day.

The Jealous Caterpillar

ONE SPRING DAY a green cater-pillar sat on a leaf. He watched a beautiful butterfly flutter past him on the breeze. "It's not fair. Here I am stuck on this boring leaf with nothing to do and nowhere to go while that lucky creature can fly across the world and see far-off lands," thought the caterpillar crossly. "And what's more," he continued to himself, "not only has that butterfly got wings with which to fly, but he's beautiful, too. Look at poor me. I'm just a dull green. No-one will notice me because I'm the same colour as the leaf." The caterpillar really did feel very sorry for himself, and rather jealous. "Go and enjoy yourself. Don't worry about me," he called spitefully to the butterfly.

But the butterfly hadn't heard a single word the caterpillar had been muttering, and soon he flew away. The caterpillar suddenly decided that he was going to be like the butterfly. "I'll learn how to fly and I'll paint myself lovely colours so that I look beautiful, too," he thought. He looked around for something to paint himself with but, of course, there was nothing at all on the leaf. Then he tried to fly. He launched himself from his leaf and tried to flap his tail, but all he did was land on the leaf below.

Along came a ladybird. "Aha!" thought the caterpillar. "Here's a beautiful creature who knows how to fly. I'll ask her to teach me." So the caterpillar said, "Hello, I've been admiring your beautiful wingcase. Could you tell me how I, too, could be beautiful? And can you teach me to fly?"

The ladybird looked at the caterpillar. "Be patient and wait a while," she said wisely, "and soon enough you'll get what you want." And with that the ladybird went on her way.

"Whatever can she mean? She's just too proud to teach me," the caterpillar thought jealously.

Some time later a bee buzzed past and landed on a nearby leaf. "Aha!" thought the caterpillar. "Here's a beautiful creature who knows how to fly. I'll ask him to

teach me." So the caterpillar said, "Hello, I've been admiring your beautiful striped back. Could you tell me how I, too, could be beautiful? And can you teach me to fly?"

The bee looked at the cater-pillar. "You'll find out soon enough,

young man," said the bee sternly.
And with that he went on his way.

"Whatever can he mean? He's
just too haughty to teach me," the
caterpillar thought jealously.

Now a while later along came a
bird. "Aha!" thought the caterpillar
once more. "Here's a beautiful
creature who knows how to fly. I'll
ask him to teach me." So once again
the caterpillar said, "Hello, I've been
admiring your beautiful feathers.
Could you tell me how I, too, could
be beautiful? And can you teach me
to fly?"

The bird looked at the caterpillar and thought to himself slyly
that here was a very silly cater-

pillar, but he would make a tasty snack for his chicks. "Let's see if I can trick him," he thought.

"I can't give you wings and I can't make you beautiful. But I can show you the world. I expect you'd like to see the world, wouldn't you, little caterpillar?" said the bird.

"Oh, yes!" said the caterpillar in great excitement.

"Climb upon my back then, little caterpillar!" said the crafty bird.

The caterpillar did as he was told and the bird flew off towards his nest. At first the caterpillar clung tightly to the bird's back but soon he felt quite sleepy and eventually he dozed off and slipped from the bird's back. Down he fell through the air and landed on a leaf, but still he didn't wake up. Soon he was wrapped in a soft, brown, papery cocoon from which he would not wake up for a long while.

Meanwhile, the bird reached his nest. "Look at the treat I've brought you," he said to his chicks.

They looked very puzzled. "What treat, Dad?" one of them piped up.

"This nice juicy caterpillar," said the bird, shaking the feathers on his back. "Climb down, little caterpillar," he said. But of course there was nothing there. Now it was the father's turn to look puzzled, while the chicks laughed at him.

"Well, I must have dropped him," he said. "I've never done that before," he added. He flew out of the nest in search of the caterpillar but he was nowhere to be seen. Once he saw a strange brown, papery parcel on a leaf, but in the end the bird had to return to the nest with his beak empty.

A long while later the caterpillar woke up. "I must get out of this stuffy wrapping," he thought, as he pushed his way out. He stood on the leaf and yawned and stretched. As he stretched, he noticed to his amazement two pairs of beautiful wings spreading out on either side of his body. "Are they really mine?" he wondered. He tried lifting and turning them and yes, he could make them work. He looked at his reflection in a raindrop and saw a lovely butterfly staring back at him.

"So the ladybird and the bee were right," he exclaimed. "How foolish I was to be a jealous caterpillar," he declared to a passing ant, "for now I am a beautiful butterfly after all."

The Lost Lion

ONCE THERE WAS a lion cub called Lenny. He was a very tiny lion cub, but he was sure that he was the bravest lion in all of Africa. When his mother taught her cubs how to stalk prey, Lenny would stalk his own mother and pounce on her. When she showed them how to wash themselves, Lenny licked his sister's face instead so that she growled at him. When the mother lioness led her cubs down to the watering hole to drink, he jumped into the water and created a huge splash that soaked everyone.

The other lionesses were not amused. "You'd better watch that

son of yours," they said to Lenny's
mother, "or he'll get into really big
trouble."

One day the mother lioness led
her cubs on their first big hunt.
"Stay close to me," she said, "or you
could get hurt."

She crawled off through the
undergrowth with her cubs following on behind, one after the other.
Lenny was at the back. The grass
tickled his tummy and he wanted to
laugh, but he was trying hard to be
obedient. So he crawled along,
making sure he kept the bobbing tail
of the cub in front in sight. On and
on they crawled until Lenny was
beginning to feel quite weary.

"But a brave lion cub doesn't give up," he thought to himself. And on he plodded.

At last the grass gave way to a clearing. Lenny looked up, and to his dismay he saw that the tail he had been following was attached, not to one of his brothers or sisters, but to a baby elephant!

Somewhere along the trail he had started following the wrong tail and now he was hopelessly lost. He wanted to cry out for his mother but then he remembered that he was the bravest lion in all of Africa.

So what do you think he did? He went straight up to the mother elephant and growled his fiercest growl at her. "That'll frighten her!" thought Lenny. "She won't dare growl back!" And, of course, she didn't growl back. Instead she lifted her trunk and trumpeted so loudly at Lenny that he was blown off his feet and through the air and landed against the hard trunk of a tree.

Lenny got up and found that his knees were knocking. "Oh my," he thought, "that elephant has a very loud growl. But I'm still

definitely the bravest lion in all of Africa." He set off across the plain. It was getting hot in the midday sun and soon Lenny began to feel sleepy. "I think I'll just take a nap in that tree," he thought, and started climbing up into the branches.

To his surprise, he found that the tree was already occupied by a large leopard. "I'll show him who's boss," thought Lenny, baring his tiny claws. The leopard raised his head to look at Lenny, and then bared his own huge, razor-sharp claws. He took a swipe at Lenny with his paw. Without even touching Lenny, the wind from the leopard's great paw swept Lenny

out of the tree and he landed with
a bump on the ground.

Lenny got up and found that
his legs were trembling. "Oh my," he
thought, "that leopard had big
claws. But I'm still definitely the
bravest lion in Africa." He set off
again across the plain. After a while
he began to feel quite hungry. "I
wonder what I can find to eat," he
thought. Just then he saw a spotted
shape lying low in the grass. "That
looks like a tasty meal," thought
Lenny as he pounced on the
spotted shape.

But the spotted shape was a
cheetah! Quick as a flash, the
cheetah sprang away and as he did

so, his tail caught Lenny a blow that sent him spinning round and round in circles.

When Lenny stopped spinning, he got up and found that his whole body was shaking. "Oh my," he thought, "that cheetah is a fast runner." Then he added in rather a small voice, "But I'm still the bravest lion in Africa."

He set off again across the plain. By now it was getting dark and Lenny was wishing he was at home with his mother and brothers and sisters. "I wonder if they've noticed I've gone," he thought sadly as a tear rolled down his furry cheek. He felt cold and tired and hungry as he crawled into the undergrowth to sleep.

Some time later Lenny was woken by a noise that was louder than anything he'd ever heard before — louder even than the elephant's trumpeting. It filled the night air and made the leaves on the trees shake. The noise was getting louder and louder and the animal that was making it was getting nearer and nearer.

Lenny peeped out from his hiding place and saw a huge golden creature with big yellow eyes that shone in the dark like lamps. It had a great crown of shaggy golden fur all around its head and its red jaws were open wide revealing a set of very large white fangs. How it roared! Lenny was terrified and about to turn tail and run, when the animal stopped roaring and spoke to him. "Come here, Lenny," said the animal gently. "It's me, your father, and I'm going to take you home. Climb up on my back, little one."

So Lenny climbed up on his father's back and was carried all the way home. And when they got there his father told his mother and his brothers and sisters that Lenny had been a very brave lion after all.

The Forgetful Squirrel

SNOW GLITTERED on the branches of the trees in Southfield Wood. Their leaves had long ago fallen, and the bare bark looked cold and grey beneath its white frosting. Down on the woodland floor, nothing moved except the occasional brown shrivelled leaf, drifting across the moss in the light breeze. The only sound was the sighing of the breeze and the far-off barking of a hungry fox.

High in the branches of an oak tree, the little squirrel slept soundly. She could not really hear the fox's cry, but still, in her sleep, she rolled herself into an even tighter, furry ball and tucked her little paws

under her chin. She had made
herself a cosy nest of twigs and
leaves, as round as a ball. Inside, she
was safe from the cold winds and
the drifting snow.

The squirrel had been asleep
since the first really cold day of
winter. Once or twice, on a very
sunny day, her little nose had
twitched, and she had peeped out
of her nest, or drey. But it was
always too cold to go hunting for
something to eat. Besides, she had
spent the summer and autumn
filling her tummy with all her
favourite foods, so that she would
be able to sleep through the winter
without a single dinner.

The little squirrel slept on through the cold months. Elsewhere in the wood, other little creatures were fast asleep as well. Meanwhile, underground, the first stirrings of life began as tiny shoots started to make their long journey to the surface.

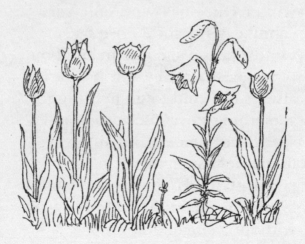

At last there came a day when the sunshine was quite warm on the branches. The snow had long ago melted away, and the sky had changed from grey to a watery blue.

The next day, the sun was even warmer, and it shone for a few minutes longer. Spring was well and truly on its way.

In her cosy drey, the little squirrel stirred. She felt the warmth of the sun trickling through the twigs and leaves of her treetop home. And she felt, too, that her tummy was just a tiny bit empty.

Poking her nose through the bottom of her nest, the little squirrel looked around at the waking world.

Far below, the first green shoots were showing under the trees. A few little animals were scurrying about among the roots and moss. The little squirrel wondered what she could find to eat so early in the year. Then she remembered something very important. Many months ago, when the nut-trees had been bowed down with shiny brown nuts, she had gathered dozens and dozens of them and stored them away for a morning just like this.

With a little chuckle, the squirrel clambered out of her nest and ran lightly along the branch. When it came to tree-climbing, she was an expert. Her clever little paws grasped the branches, while her big furry tail helped her to balance as she leapt without hesitation from branch to branch. However high she climbed, the little squirrel felt no fear. The treetops were her home, and she was happy there.

But the little squirrel had not hidden her nuts in the treetops. She had dug several little holes in the ground and buried her store here and there in the forest. Now all she had to do was to find one of these stores and enjoy her first meal of the year.

The little squirrel skipped happily down the trunk of the tree and looked around. She knew that one of her secret hiding places was not very far.

But, oh dear, how different things looked after the winter snows. The little squirrel remembered that her store was near a small bush with bright red and orange leaves. But now the leaves had all disappeared. Every bush was a mass of bare twigs. It was impossible to tell them apart.

Then the little squirrel remembered something else. There had been some red and white spotted toadstools near her hiding place. She looked eagerly around, but the clump of toadstools had also disappeared.

For the first time, the little squirrel began to feel worried. What if she couldn't find any of her nuts? What would she eat? How could she survive until spring had properly arrived?

All too soon, the light began to fade. Knowing that it would soon be cold and dark, the little squirrel hurried back to her home, where she could curl up, warm and safe, until morning.

"I'll worry about where my nut-store is then," she said to herself. "Tonight I will have a good sleep, so that I am ready to search tomorrow."

But in the morning, the little squirrel had no more idea where she had stored her food than she had had the night before.

"Perhaps I will be able to see where the ground has been disturbed," thought the little squirrel. But even as the thought crossed her mind, she recalled vividly how carefully she had patted the earth back into place after each burial.

"I have been too clever," said

the little squirrel. "What am I going to do?"

All day long, the hungry creature scampered through the wood. She was so worried about her food-stores now that she was not very careful to look out for danger. That is why, as she bounded around the base of a mighty oak tree, she came face to face with a long, lean, reddish creature. It was the fox!

Now foxes do not often catch squirrels, for they are not good climbers, but no hungry fox is going to give up the chance of supper when it comes leaping towards him. With one swift

movement, the fox caught hold of the little squirrel's tail in his strong jaws.

"Where are you off to?" he asked between clenched teeth.

"I'm … I'm … I'm searching for my food-stores," said the little squirrel in a rush. The poor little animal was so frightened that she said the first thing that came into her head, which happened to be the truth.

"Food-stores?" queried the fox, for at least one of those words was of very great interest to him at the moment. "And what might be in these food-stores?"

"Oh, um, rabbits," said the

squirrel, thinking as fast as she could. "Rabbits and chickens and one or two ducks."

The very mention of those creatures made the fox's mouth water. They were much more to his liking than squirrel, which in fact he had never tasted.

"And where exactly are these food-stores?" he enquired.

The little squirrel had her wits about her now.

"They are here somewhere," she said. "But I can't quite remember which tree I hid them under. It will take me weeks to find them, but with your strong paws and digging expertise, you will be able to unearth them in a few minutes. I think that this tree is the best place to start."

The fox had begun digging before he had even had a chance to think about what the squirrel had said. Somehow the mention of chickens and rabbits and ducks had muddled his usually sharp brain.

The digging was much slower than usual because the fox had to keep a tight grip on the squirrel's tail, but before long he had dug quite a deep hole under the oak tree.

There was nothing there at all.

"Then it might be this tree," said the squirrel, pointing to a nearby trunk.

The fox felt that he had very little to lose. After all, if he did not find the food-store, at least he had a plump little squirrel for his supper.

But the second hole was empty as well.

"One more," growled the fox between his teeth, "and then I'm going to eat you!"

The fox began to dig his third hole, and it did not take him long to come upon a whole mass of little round, brown shiny objects.

The fox could not believe his eyes. He felt a great anger rising up inside him and he opened his mouth in a mighty shout.

"NUTS?" he bellowed. "What good are nuts to ME?"

But, of course, when he opened his mouth, the little squirrel was able to jump free, and in ten seconds flat, she had scampered to the top of the nearest tree.

"They're terribly good for you!" she called down cheekily. "A nut a day keeps the doctor away, that's what I always say."

The fox was absolutely furious. He chased his tail round and round the tree to relieve his feelings. Then he sat down to wait with a very determined expression on his foxy face.

"Little squirrel," he called, "I'm going to wait here until you come down. You can't stay up there for ever."

"No," called the squirrel, "but I can jump to another tree, just look at me!" And spreading her beautiful tail out behind her, she leapt across the clearing to the tree opposite.

Now, the fox could not sit at the bottom of every tree in the wood, and anyway, his tummy, which had been empty, now felt as hollow as a cave. Muttering fiercely, he slunk away in search of food.

As for the little squirrel, she had found her first food-store — or at least the fox had. She ran down the tree and quickly gathered up as many nuts as she could carry.

The squirrel never did find all her stores, but the nuts she hid and lost grew into new nut-trees, so they fed her daughters and her granddaughters. And they were much better at remembering things, I'm happy to say.

The Sleepy Teddy Bear

ADAM HAD a beautiful teddy bear called Mr Muffle. He had lovely golden fur and two bright little eyes. Adam's grandmother thought he looked a little chilly one winter's day, so she knitted him a bright red sweater. Adam felt that he was a very special teddy bear indeed.

Mr Muffle had lots of jobs to do. He kept an eye on things in Adam's room during the day, when Adam was out and about. He warmed up Adam's bed in the evening, ready for him to jump into after his bath. And *just* before Adam got into bed, Mr Muffle had his most important task of all. He had to check under the bed for *monsters*. Adam had once read a story about a monster who lived under a little boy's bed. The more he read about it, the more likely it seemed to him that the fluffy, dark space under his bed was just the kind of place that a monster might love to live. And you never knew when a monster might move in. That was why Mr Muffles had to look under the bed *every* night.

When Mr Muffles had checked very carefully under the bed (and had a quick look behind the curtains as well, just to be on the safe side), Adam was happy to cuddle down between the sheets and go to sleep. He didn't need his bedroom door to be a ajar or a night light on his bedside table. He knew that he was as safe as he could be with Mr Muffles beside him.

One evening in late autumn, when it was already dark outside, Adam's mother looked at the clock and told him it was time for his bath and bed. Adam was in the middle of playing with his new space game, so he pretended not to hear her.

"Adam!" called his mother. "I know you can hear me, even on Mars. Put your toys away now and get ready for bed. We're already quite late this evening."

"All right, Mum," said Adam, reluctantly. He really didn't feel like going to bed yet. As he was putting the pieces of his space game back in the box, one of them rolled under the table, and Adam gave it another nudge with his foot.

"Mum," he said, "I can't go yet. I've lost one of the pieces of my game. I must find it before I go to bed or … or … I won't be able to sleep because I'll be worried."

"All right," sighed Adam's mother, and she got down on her hands and knees to help him look for the missing piece.

It took quite a long time to find the piece under the table, partly because Adam managed to "search" between his mother and the table most of the time, but at last it was found.

"Now hurry up!" said Mum. "It's

an hour past your bedtime. Just a quick bath, Adam, and no more delays please."

Adam felt a little bit guilty as he scampered up the stairs. He thought for a moment about "losing" one of the ducks from his bath, but he was beginning to be quite tired now.

The sleepy boy had his bath in double-quick time. I'm pretty sure that there were lots of parts of him that were not much cleaner after his bath than they were before it. (Adam never was very keen on washing his *ears*, for example!)

When Adam went into his bedroom, he knew at once that

something was different. In fact, something was more than different — it was *wrong*! It took him a moment to realise what the problem was.

Mr Muffles was asleep! Yes, the teddy bear in the red sweater was sitting in his usual place on the bed, but there was no doubt about it, those bright little beady eyes were closed. A tiny snoring sound came from Mr Muffles' furry chest.

Adam climbed into bed and clutched Mr Muffles, who did not wake up.

"Goodnight!" said Adam's mother from the doorway. "Go straight to sleep now! And goodnight, Mr Muffles!"

"But Mum!" called Adam. "Mr Muffles is already asleep!"

"I'm not surprised," said his mother. "Have you seen what the time is? All boys and their bears should be fast asleep by now. Goodnight!"

Well, Adam settled down into his bed. He felt more sleepy than ever, but every time he closed his eyes, a worrying thought would pop into his mind.

Mr Muffles hadn't checked under the bed. What if there was something green and hairy under there, just waiting until he was asleep? Or, worse still, what if there was something purple and slimy under there, ready to ooze across the carpet as soon as the coast was clear? Or what about something brown and prickly, with very sharp teeth?

Adam could feel a tingling at the tips of his toes, just where a monster might decide to nibble first on its midnight snack.

Adam gave Mr Muffles a little shake. "Wake up!" he whispered. "Mr Muffles! Wake up!" But the silly old teddy bear just carried on sleeping.

Adam tried very hard to be sensible. "There was no monster under the bed last night," he said to himself, "and no monster the night before that, *or* the night before that. In fact, there has *never* been a monster under the bed, so there won't be one now."

Still, at the back of his mind, a little voice was saying, "You don't *know* that there isn't a monster tonight, because nobody has checked to see. And it *would* be the very night that nobody checked when a monster might come."

Adam lay awake in the darkness and listened very carefully. He was almost sure he could hear a sort of scrabbling, scratching, snorting sound coming from you-know-where. And wasn't that a slobbering, squelching, sucking kind of noise, coming from somewhere down by his toes?

Adam decided to be brave. He switched on the bedside light and got out of bed. If Mr Muffles had the courage to look under the bed, then so did he.

First Adam rummaged in his chest of drawers for his torch. It was true that Mr Muffles didn't use a torch, but then bear eyes are much sharper than human ones, as everyone knows.

Adam found his torch and turned it on. He knelt down very quietly and took a deep breath.

What was best? To snatch up the corner of the quilt and have one quick look? Or to lift the quilt gently, gently and very slowly peep under the bed? Adam couldn't make up his mind. Mr Muffles did one quick look, but then he was used to the job. Adam felt that a beginner should perhaps move more slowly — to make sure he did the job thoroughly, of course.

So very, very slowly, Adam bent down, and very, very gently, he lifted up the corner of his quilt. Bending closer, he peered into the space under the bed, into the dusty dark.

"Aaaaaaaagh!" yelled Adam, as he realised what he was seeing.

"Aaaaaaaagh!" yelled the monster, blinking its yellow eyes.

Yes, there *was* a monster under the bed, and it looked just as frightened as Adam was!

Now all the time that Adam had been getting ready to look under the bed, he had only half believed there might be a monster. If you had asked him to say whether, in his heart of hearts, he really

thought there was a monster under his bed, then he would have said, "No, of course not. No one *really* has monsters *anywhere.*"

But here he was, face to face with a monster. Adam rubbed his eyes. The easiest reason for seeing a monster might be that he was already asleep. But Adam was awake all right. He was particularly sure after he had rubbed his eyes, because he had forgotten that he was still holding the torch and he managed to clonk himself on the forehead with it.

"Oooooh!" said the monster, sympathetically.

Adam smiled. It was really quite

a friendly looking monster, even if it did have green spots and funny purple hair.

The monster smiled. He had a lot of rather sharp-looking little teeth, but then so do kittens, and everyone thinks *they* are cute.

"I'm a monster," said the monster, "in case you didn't realise." He had quite a high-pitched, squeaky little voice.

"I'm Adam," said Adam. "I'm a boy," he added, in case the monster wasn't very used to humans. "Er … have you lived here long?"

"Oh, a few months now," said the monster carelessly. "It's a very nice bed to live under. The last one

I had was always being swept and cleaned. You know, there is nothing in the world that monsters hate more than vacuum cleaners. Ugh!"

"What else is under there?" asked Adam curiously, peering past the monster.

"Well, now, this is my private place, so I think that's *my* business," said the monster, primly. "But if you're thinking about that football sock you lost, yes, it is here, and no, you can't have it back."

"All right," said Adam. "I've got some new ones now, anyway."

Adam tried to think what his next question should be, but really he had so many, he hardly knew where to begin. Then he thought of something that was really quite important. The trouble was, it was quite a delicate matter, too.

"I was wondering," said Adam, "whether you have everything you need under there. You know, food and so on?"

"You want to know if I'm going to eat you," said the monster, with a nasty little giggle but a rather nice smile.

"Well, I did wonder," said Adam, trying to look as if he didn't mind very much one way or the other. "What *do* monsters eat these days?"

The monster giggled again. "Don't worry," he said, "I survive very nicely on the odd spider that crawls down the corner. Delicious!"

Adam felt a little better after that, but it didn't seem right, somehow, just to get back into bed and go to sleep. He wondered if he really would be able to sleep, *knowing* that there was a monster under the bed, however friendly it was.

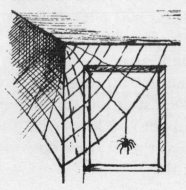

Just then, Adam heard a little snuffling sound. It was Mr Muffles, waking up at last! With a soft thud, Mr Muffles landed on the floor beside Adam. The sleepy teddy bear took in the situation at a glance.

"Ah," he said, "I see that you two have met."

Adam felt strongly that Mr Muffles had some explaining to do. After all, he had been failing in his most important job.

"Night after night, Mr Muffles," said Adam, "you promised me that there were no monsters under my bed. And yet you knew that there was at least one! How do you explain that?"

"Now, Adam," said Mr Muffles, trying to sound like an old and wise bear, "I never actually said that there were no monsters. *You* said, 'Is everything all right under the bed?' and I said, 'Yes!' As you can see, it was all right. It's just that there is a little tiny monster there as well."

"But how did you know it was all right?" asked Adam. "How did you know he wasn't a really very dangerous monster, who might crunch teddy bears and leave only their ears on the pillow in the morning?"

"*Please*, said Mr Muffles, "do give me credit for some sense. The monster and I have had some long chats while you were asleep. I was quite sure that no harm would come to us."

"And what do we do now?" asked Adam. "That's what I'd like to know."

"I can quite see," said Mr Muffles, "that from your point of view things are rather different now. Sleeping with a monster under the bed that you don't know is there is a very different matter from sleeping with a monster under the bed that you *do* know is there. Do you think you could ever get used to the idea, Adam?"

"I don't think so," said Adam. "It doesn't feel right, somehow."

"Very well," said Mr Muffles, then I have another idea.

If you were to creep into Adam's room tonight, you would see a very strange sight. Adam and the monster sleep *in* the bed, and

Adam finds that the monster is every bit as cuddly as Mr Muffles. The teddy bear sleeps *under* the bed, so that he can make sure that no new monsters try to take over the space during the night. During the day, they swap over.

So remember, a monster under the bed is not the end of the world, but do make sure your teddy bear is doing his job properly each night, won't you?

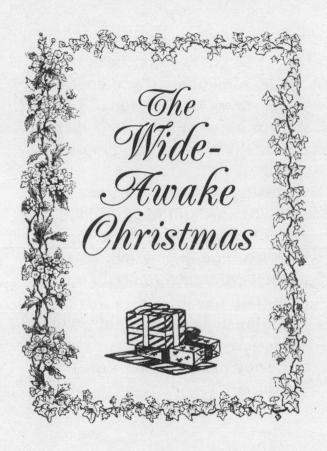

The Wide-Awake Christmas

USUALLY, it's not too difficult to get to sleep, but sometimes, if you are feeling poorly, or worried about something, or very excited, then it can be the hardest thing in the world.

Every year on Christmas Eve, twins Tommy and Joe just could not get to sleep. All night long, they would be running along the landing to their parents' room with one important question.

"Has he been yet?" they would ask eagerly.

They meant Father Christmas, of course.

Daddy would groan and turn

over. Mummy would call out.

"Go back to bed, Tommy and Joe. You'll be so tired in the morning, you won't be able to stay awake to open your presents *if* Father Christmas brings you any. I don't know what he'll have to say about two such naughty little boys."

"Oh, don't tell him! Don't tell him! We'll be good!" cried Tommy and Joe.

"We don't have to tell him," growled Daddy. "He knows *everything*. You just watch out."

And the twins would scamper back to bed and try ever so hard to shut their eyes and fall asleep. But it was *so* difficult.

Twenty minutes later, there would be little feet skipping across the landing again and right into Mummy's and Daddy's big bedroom.

"Has he been yet?" the little boys would whisper, tugging at the quilt.

"He *did* come," their father would whisper back, "but he heard that two bad little boys were not asleep, so he went away again. He *may* come back, but only if you shut your eyes and *keep* them shut."

As fast as their little legs would carry them, the boys would hurry back to their beds. But did they go straight to sleep until morning? Oh no. Ten minutes later they were off again. This time the question was different.

"Is it morning yet?" asked Joe.

Daddy muttered and mumbled and sat right up in bed.

"Do *you* think it's morning?" he said, looking at the bedside light. Its hands were glowing in the dark. They said half past three.

"It might be," said Tommy, hopefully. "Then we can open our

presents.

"It's *dark*," moaned Daddy. "It's the middle of the night. It's ages and ages and ages until morning. *Go* back to bed and don't come back until you can see that it's getting light outside. Do you understand, both of you?"

Tommy and Joe nodded their heads and went back to their room. But did they snuggle back into bed? Oh no. They stood on tiptoes so that they could see out of the window. They wanted to be ready the very *moment* it began to get light.

It was a pity that a tree blowing in the wind made the next-door neighbour's outside light come on only fifteen minutes later.

Mummy and Daddy were drifting back to sleep when … *woomph! … woomph! …* two little bodies jumped right in the middle of their tummies.

"It's morning. It is! It is!" shouted the boys, bouncing up and down.

I'm afraid that what Daddy said then is really not repeatable. Luckily it was muffled by the quilt. Five seconds later, two little boys were being dragged unceremoniously across the landing and plonked …*one! … two! …* in their beds.

"If I hear a peep out of either

of you in the next three hours, I won't answer for my actions," yawned Daddy, pulling the curtains firmly shut and making the fiercest face he could.

What do you think happened? I won't go into the details, but by half past four, Mummy and Daddy had given up and were hugging cups of coffee in the sitting room, while two excited little boys opened a wonderful pile of presents.

Sometimes, you just have to give in gracefully.

When it was nearly time for the next Christmas, however, Daddy put his foot down.

"Now, I want a word with you boys," he said. "You know we have Granny coming to stay with us this Christmas. She's an old lady, and she won't want to be woken up in the middle of the night. You could make her very ill. You are both big boys now, so I want you to promise me that you won't come out of your room until it is morning. You've got your own big teddy bear clock now. When the little hand is pointing straight down and the big hand is pointing straight up, you can get up. That's still very early, but it isn't the middle of the night. Now, is it a deal?"

"Yes, Daddy," said Joe.

"Yes, Daddy," said Tommy.

The boys loved their granny. They certainly wouldn't want to do anything to upset her.

To the twins' parents, it seemed as if Christmas Eve arrived far too quickly. To the boys, the days

seemed to crawl past. But at last it was here, and daddy went to collect Granny from the station.

"Happy Christmas, boys!" she called, as she came through the front door. Tommy and Joe couldn't help noticing that she had two bulging bags of presents and a suitcase that looked as if it was about to burst.

That evening, the whole family had a special Christmas Eve supper, with crackers and candles. The boys were almost unbearably excited.

"Now, it's bedtime for you two," said Mummy at last.

"Goodnight, boys," smiled Daddy. "Now, remember what I said, won't you?"

"Goodnight, darlings," said Granny. And, much to their surprise, she winked at them, careful that Daddy shouldn't see.

Tommy and Joe went to their bedroom and put on their pyjamas. They climbed into their beds and turned off the light. A few moments passed.

"Are you asleep?" whispered Tommy to his twin.

"No," whispered Joe, "are you?"

The boys lay staring into the darkness. They could just see the luminous hands of their teddy bear clock. It was *hours* until the hands would be pointing straight up and straight down.

Time passed *so* slowly. It almost seemed as though the hands of the clock were going backwards! There was no way that the boys could get to sleep.

"This is going to be a *long* night," groaned Joe.

Later still, the twins heard their parents saying goodnight to Granny on the landing. The little strip of light at the bottom of the door disappeared as the landing light was turned off. Then there was silence.

More long, long minutes passed. The house was very, very quiet. Then the boys heard a funny little rustling sound and a tiny squeak as someone turned the handle of their door.

"Are you awake, boys?" said Granny's voice quietly.

"No!' whispered the twins.

"Good!" said Granny, coming into the room. "I don't know about you, but I never can get to sleep on Christmas Eve. It's much too exciting. I thought perhaps we could open one or two little presents to make the time pass more quickly. But you've got to promise to be very, very quiet. We don't want to wake up you-know-who, *do* we?"

Well, Granny and the twins had

a wonderful time. Some of the presents were games to play, and it was even more fun playing and trying to be as quiet as mice at the same time.

Granny had sensibly brought one or two little Christmas snacks as well.

"Just to keep us going," she giggled, opening a tin of sausage rolls and cheese straws.

Unfortunately, they were all three having such a good time, they didn't keep an eye on the clock. It was still dark when the big hand finally pointed straight up and the little hand pointed straight down.

Granny and the boys didn't

notice the door silently opening.

"Mother!" cried Daddy. "You really are the limit!" But he was laugh-ing until tears streamed down his face.

"You know the worst thing?" said Daddy later, when they were all downstairs. "Granny would never have let *me* open my presents early, when I was little!"

"Well," smiled his mother, "that's why *grannies* have more fun."

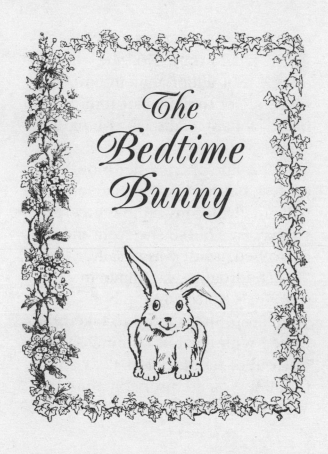

The Bedtime Bunny

CAROLINE'S MOTHER shook her head firmly. "No," she said. "Not under any circumstances. Not tonight. Not tomorrow night. Not any night. Do you understand?"

Caroline opened her mouth to protest, but her mother had her I-will-not-change-my-mind-whatever-you-say face on, so she went meekly off to bed. It just wasn't fair.

The trouble was all about Caroline's fluffy white rabbit, Snowdrop. She wanted to take him to bed with her, but Mummy said it was out of the question. Poor Caroline, you are probably thinking. Why shouldn't she have her toy rabbit it bed with her? But Snowdrop wasn't a toy rabbit. He was real!

"Rabbits are cuddly and friendly, I know," Caroline's mother had said, "but, darling, they're not indoor animals. They belong outside. Snowdrop might make a terrible mess in your bedroom, and he really wouldn't be happy, you know."

Caroline was quite, quite sure her mother was wrong. Darling Snowdrop was always so pleased to see her when she went out to his hutch with a few green cabbage leaves.

He liked to play, too, when she let him out of his hutch for a hop around the garden. She had to be very careful that he didn't hop right away, but that wasn't because he didn't like her, that was because he was a very adventurous bunny.

Caroline sat in her bedroom and felt close to tears. It was a cold night, and she felt sure that Snowdrop would much rather be with her in her warm little bed. So do you know what that naughty

little girl did? She waited until she could hear that her mother was watching television downstairs, then she put on her slippers and dressing gown and crept out of the back door, taking her little torch with her.

Snowdrop seemed rather surprised to see her. Although the wind was whistling around his cage, he looked quite cosy and comfortable curled up in his pile of straw. In fact, when Caroline put her hands in to pick him up, he didn't really seem to want to come.

"You'll like it, Snowdrop, really you will," said the little girl. "But you mustn't make a noise as we go upstairs. All right?"

Caroline and her rabbit slipped through the back door and shut it carefully behind them. The little girl crept up the stairs as quietly as she could, which was quite difficult because Snowdrop would keep struggling. At last they were safely in Caroline's bedroom, with the door shut behind them.

Clutching her rabbit tightly, the little girl snuggled down in bed and stretched out her hand to turn off the light. It should have been lovely, drifting off to sleep with her cuddly bunny in her arms, but, oh dear, Snowdrop was the *wriggliest* rabbit you have ever come across. And he was quite strong too. He wriggled and he jiggled and in the end he kicked Caroline so hard with his big back feet that she said, "Oh!" and let go of him.

With a *thump!* Snowdrop landed on the floor. Caroline heard him hopping off towards her toy cupboard before she had a chance to turn on the light. Quickly, the little girl jumped out of bed and ran across the room to catch her rabbit.

"Come here, Snowdrop!" she called, as loudly as she dared. But Snowdrop was already knocking toys over and crashing around in the cupboard. Then he started to nibble the straw-stuffed paws of the little girl's favourite teddy bear!

Just then Mummy, who had been on her way upstairs and thought she heard a strange noise, popped her head round the door.

"Why is your light still on?" she asked. "Come on, darling. You've got school tomorrow."

Caroline swung round guiltily. She must make sure that her mother didn't see Snowdrop.

"I'm just getting into bed again, Mum," she said. "I just couldn't sleep because ... because ... because the wind was so loud."

Mummy looked at Caroline more suspiciously than she had done before. "No, it isn't," she said. "What's going on in here?"

"Nothing," said Caroline, but she couldn't help taking a quick look towards the cupboard.

Caroline's mother didn't need any more clues. She strode over to the cupboard and flung the doors wide open.

There was nothing to be seen. Mummy peered here and there, but she couldn't see anything strange. Caroline held her breath. Snowdrop was being so good and quiet.

Then Mummy frowned and wrinkled up her nose.

"What's that *smell*?" she asked. "Something in this cupboard smells extraordinarily like a ... fluffy ... white ... *rabbit*!"

Just at that moment, Snowdrop hopped right out of the cupboard, leaving the smell, a half-chewed teddy bear, a scratched toy train and a squashed puppet behind him. At first Mummy was really cross. Then she calmed down a little and said that she supposed there were some things that everyone just had to find out for themselves.

"Do you think Snowdrop was happy in your bed?" she asked.

"No," said Caroline.

"Do you think he was happy in your toy cupboard?"

"Well," said Caroline, "I think he did have quite a good time, yes, I do."

"And are *you* happy that he was in your toy cupboard?"

Caroline looked at the chewed teddy bear and damaged toys.

"No, not really," she whispered.

"Are you happy that you're going to have to clean everything in your cupboard and find out where that smell is coming from?" asked Mummy.

Caroline wrinkled her nose. "No, I'm not," she said.

"Are you happy that you didn't do what I said and told me stories when I came to see what was happening?"

"No." Caroline hung her head.

Mummy smiled and kissed her little girl.

"One more question, honey," she said.

"Where do you think rabbits really like to sleep?"

Caroline smiled. "In their hutches," she said, "outside."

I think she's right. Don't you?

The Dream Merchant

ONCE UPON A TIME, there was a little boy who had the most wonderful dreams. His name was David. Every night when he closed his eyes, it was as though he walked into a wonderful new world. But David's dreams didn't just come to him by chance. He bought them from the dream merchant, who visited him as soon as his eyes were closed. And the dream merchant had his price, as you will see.

It happened like this. One day, David had been rather lazy at school. He didn't pay attention during his lessons, and the teacher spoke to him sharply.

"Do you have nice dreams at

night, David?" she enquired, in front of the whole class.

"Sometimes," said David, looking puzzled.

"Then I'm surprised you need to dream during the day as well," said the teacher. "Perhaps your night-time dreams aren't exciting enough. I shall have to send the dream merchant to you."

Of course, all the children wanted to know what she meant, but the teacher just smiled mysteriously and would say nothing more.

That night, David went to bed as usual and fell asleep so quickly that he didn't even have time to turn his bedside lamp off.

"Good evening," said a magical voice in his ear.

David felt as though he was awake, although he knew he was really asleep.

"Good evening," he replied.

"I'm the dream merchant," said the voice. "A friend of mine told me that you might like a visit. What kind of dream would you like to have?"

"Isn't this already a dream?" asked David.

"Oh," said the dream merchant, "everything is a dream in a way. It depends how you look at it. Have you thought yet? What would you like to dream about tonight?"

"Could I dream about pirates?" asked David, who had been reading a very exciting book on just that subject.

"Of course," said the dream merchant. "Would you like an exciting dream, a scary dream, a comfortable dream, or a dream full of wonders?"

David wasn't sure. "I'd like an exciting dream," he said, "but could I have some … um … wonders as well?"

"No, no, only one kind at a time. You can have wonders tomorrow night if you like. An exciting dream it is. Now, what would you like to pay?"

"Pay?" echoed David. "What do you mean?"

"Well, I'm a merchant," said the magical voice a little impatiently. "I don't *give* things away, you know. I need something from you in return."

"What kind of something?" asked David.

"A whole day of paying attention at school, or a whole week of doing what your mother says, or a whole

month of making your bed properly.
Which shall it be?"

David didn't hesitate. "I'll pay
attention at school tomorrow," he
said. With that, David heard a *woosh!*
and a *whizz!* and he found himself
on the deck of a pirate ship.

When David woke the next
morning, he found that his lamp was

still on, with his pirate book lying beside it. His head was spinning from the amazing adventures he had had during the night.

That day at school, he started work on his pirate project, and the teacher was delighted with the way he concentrated and had such imaginative ideas.

"It's exciting, isn't it?" she said, but whether she meant the project or the visit of the dream merchant, David wasn't sure.

After that, the dream merchant came every night. In exchange for marvellous dreams, David helped his father in the garden and stopped teasing his little sister.

He continued to pay attention at school. He was surprised to find that everything seemed to work a hundred times better when he just tried a tiny bit harder. And so it was that a night came when the dream merchant visited as usual.

David asked for a dream about castles, and the dream merchant was happy to oblige. But when it came to thinking of a suitable payment, there was a problem. Everything the dream merchant suggested was something that David did already.

"You know," said David. "I've learnt that doing my best at things makes me happier all the time. I do it anyway, even if I don't have a dream to pay for."

"Then I think my work is done," said the dream merchant, with a smile in his voice. "From now on, you can make your own dreams. In fact, most of the time you can do anything at all that you want to do. You just have to try, that's all."

You could try it too. It's true!

Bobby's Best Birthday Present

IT WAS the morning of Bobby's birthday and he was very excited. When he came down to breakfast, there on the table was a big pile of presents. Bobby opened them one by one. There was a beautiful book with pictures of wild animals, a toy racing car and a baseball cap.

Bobby was very pleased with his presents, but where was the present from his parents? "Close your eyes and hold out your hands!" said his mother. When he opened his eyes there was a large rectangular parcel in his hands. Bobby tore off the wrapping and inside was a box. And inside the

box was a wonderful, shiny, electric
train set.

For a moment, Bobby looked at
the train set lying in the box. It was
so lovely he could hardly bear to
touch it. There was an engine and six
carriages all lying neatly on their

sides. Bobby carefully lifted the engine out of the box. Then he set up the track and soon he had the train whizzing round his bedroom floor. Freddie the cat came in and watched the train going round. Round and round she watched it go, then one time when the train came past her she swiped at it with her paw and derailed it. The engine and the six carriages came tumbling off the track and landed in a heap on the floor. "Look what you've done!" wailed Bobby as he picked up the train and reassembled it. The carriages were undamaged, but the engine had hit the side of his bed and was badly dented.

Bobby was very upset. "My brand new train is ruined!" he cried.

"Don't worry, Bobby," said his mother, "we can't take it back to the shop now, but we can take it to the toymender in the morning. I'm sure he'll make a good job of mending the engine and it'll look as good as new again." Bobby played with his racing car, he wore his new baseball cap and he read his new book, but really all he wanted to do was to play with his train set. He went to bed that night with the engine on the floor near his bed.

In the morning when Bobby woke up, the first thing he did was to look at the poor broken engine of his train set. He picked it up, expecting to see the buckled metal, but the engine was perfect. He couldn't believe his eyes! He ran to his parents. "Look, look!" he cried. They were as amazed as he was. The engine worked perfectly and Bobby played happily with his train set all day — but he made sure Freddie kept out of his room!

That night Bobby couldn't sleep. He lay in bed tossing and turning. Then he heard a noise. It was the sound of his train set rushing round the track. He peered into the darkness and yes, he could definitely make out the shape of the train as it sped by. How had the train started?

It couldn't start all by itself! Had
Freddie crept into his room and
flicked the switch? As his eyes
gradually became accustomed to the
dark Bobby could make out several
shapes in the carriages. Who were
the mysterious passengers? He slid
out of bed and on to the floor beside
the train set. Now he could see that
the passengers were little folk
wearing strange pointed hats and
leafy costumes. "Elves!" thought
Bobby.

At that moment one of the elves
spotted Bobby. "Hello there!" he
called as the train rushed past again.
"We saw that your train set was
broken. We so much wanted a ride

that we fixed it. I hope you don't mind!" Bobby was too astounded to say anything at all. "Come with us for a ride," called the elf as his carriage approached again.

As the train passed him the elf leaned out of the carriage and

grabbed Bobby by the hand. Bobby felt himself shrinking as he flew through the air, and the next instant he was sitting beside the elf in the carriage of his very own train set! "Here we go — hold tight!" called the elf as the train left the track and went out through the window into the night sky.

"Now, where would you like to go? What would you like to see?" asked the elf.

"Toyland!" replied Bobby without hesitation. Sure enough, the train headed towards a track which curved up a mountain made of pink and white sugar. Beside the track were toys going about their daily business. Bobby saw a ragdoll getting into a shiny tin car. Then a wooden sailor puppet wound up the car with a large key and off went the doll. He saw three teddy bears setting off for school with their satchels on their backs. Then he saw a brightly coloured clown playing a drum.

The train stopped and Bobby and the elves got out. "Now for some fun!" said one of the elves. They had come to a halt by a toy fairground. Bobby found that this was like no other fairground he had ever been to before. For in Toyland, all the rides are real. The horses on the carousel were real horses. The dodgem cars were real cars. And when he got in the rocket for the rocket ride, it took him all the way to the moon and back!

"Time to go, Bobby," said one of the elves at last. "It'll be morning soon." Bobby climbed wearily back into the train and soon he was fast asleep. When he woke up it was morning, and he was back in his

bed. The train set lay quite still on its tracks. But in one of the carriages was a scrap of paper and on the paper, in tiny spidery writing, were the words: *We hope you enjoyed your trip to Toyland — the elves.*

The Every-Year Dolls

DIANA PICKED UP her last Christmas present. She had opened all the rest, and they had been full of wonderful surprises. But this present was different.

"I don't really need to open this," she said. "After all, we know exactly what's going to be inside it."

"Well, not *exactly*," her mother protested. "I do know what you mean, darling, but it is very, very kind of Granny to make a special present for you each year, especially now that her eyesight is not so good. And her fingers are not as nimble as they were, you know."

Diana did know, and she tried hard to be grateful, but it really was very hard. She couldn't help sighing as she undid the brightly coloured paper.

It had all started when Diana was three. Granny had made her a beautiful little doll, with a yellow satin skirt and a bright blue top. She had black silky hair and little red boots, and the smiliest, jolliest face you could imagine. Diana had really loved that little doll, the tiniest of the dolls she had. It was partly because she was so small and partly because Granny had made her specially — just for her.

Of course, both Diana and her mother had told Granny how very pleased she was with her present.

Perhaps they had said so just one time too many, for the next year, Granny made another doll. It was exactly the same as the first doll, except that this time it had a pink skirt and a white top and little blue boots. Oh, and its hair was golden.

Diana quite liked having sister dolls. They looked just right sitting either side of the table in her dolls' house. She told Granny how pleased she was — and she meant it. Granny smiled and admired the dolls' house.

But the next year, when Diana was five, Granny made her *another* doll. It was exactly the same as the first two, but with different coloured clothes again and red hair this time.

"For the dolls' house," wrote Granny on the card that came with the carefully wrapped parcel.

As the years went by, Granny became more and more frail. She could not travel to see her granddaughter any more, but she still made dolls. Each Christmas a similar parcel arrived, and each time there was a little doll inside, almost, but not exactly, like the very first one.

Diana still wrote a nice letter each year, thanking her Granny. She knew that it took the old lady longer and longer each time to make the doll, but each one was as perfect as the one before. Diana was rather old now to play with dolls, and the last thing she wanted for Christmas was *another* of the every-year dolls, as she called them, but she didn't want to hurt the old lady's feelings if she could help it.

The very last doll didn't arrive at Christmas. It was the twelfth doll, and Diana was fourteen. Granny was very ill that winter. At the end of November, a telephone call came to say that Granny had passed away peacefully in her own home. A few weeks after Christmas, Diana's mother travelled to Granny's house to sort out her things and make preparations for its sale. She found the twelfth doll, almost complete, in Granny's workbasket. Only its eyes, nose and mouth had not yet been added.

Diana's mother brought her the last doll. "I know Granny would have wanted you to have it, darling," she said.

It was many years since Diana had seen Granny. She felt a little bit sad because her mother was sad, but she did not really miss the old lady. And she certainly did not miss the every-year dolls. She put the last doll, with the others, in the box that contained some of the toys she had played with as a child, and soon forgot all about them.

Almost twenty years passed. Diana went to college and worked hard. She became a doctor and worked even harder. Then she got married and had a little girl of her own — and she worked harder still.

In all that time, Diana had not thought about her box of toys, but one day, watching her baby daughter playing with a new plastic doll, she suddenly thought of the box tucked away in the attic. When the baby was in bed, she found the box and brought it downstairs.

As she opened the box, Diana felt the years slip away. One by one, she took out the little dolls, but now she looked at them with different eyes. She noticed for the first time how beautifully they were made. The stitches were tiny. The fabrics were soft and in lovely colours. Best of all were the tiny faces, each with its own laughing expression. For the first time in years, Diana thought of her Granny and all the patience and love that had gone into each tiny doll. Tears came to her eyes.

It was almost Christmas again, and Diana could not bear to put the dolls away again. Her own little girl was much too small to play with them — they were so perfect and fragile.

Diana picked up the dolls one by one and put them side by side along the mantelpiece. Their outstretched arms touched each other, as though the twelve little dolls were holding hands. They looked lovely.

As Diana stood and looked at the dolls, her husband came into the room. Glancing at the mantelpiece he said, "Oh, you've started putting the Christmas decorations up. How lovely!"

Diana smiled. It was only a few weeks before Christmas. Now she knew exactly what to do with the little dolls.

That evening, Diana carefully sewed the dolls together, so that one little hand clasped the next. Last of all, she found some embroidery thread and gently put two eyes, a little nose, and a mouth on the last little doll. She took a long time over it, for she wanted it to be just as fine as the other dolls. Then she pinned up the string of dolls above the mantelpiece, where they looked as bright and colourful as any Christmas decoration.

As Diana's baby grew older, she noticed that the dolls were put in the same place each Christmas.

"They're so pretty," she said. "Where did they come from?"

So Diana told her the story of the twelve little dolls.

"And will we have them *every* year?" asked the little girl.

"Of course," said Diana. "They are every-year dolls — and always will be."

The Surprise Box

ONCE THERE WAS an annoying little boy who had a habit of guessing what was in the presents he was given each year for his birthday. You can imagine what it was like. A kindly aunt would come to visit, holding a present with bright wrapping paper and a ribbon tied in a great big bow.

"Happy birthday, Robert," she would say. "I hope you like this."

Robert would take the present, shake it, prod it, pass it from hand to

hand and, without undoing it, say, "Oh, it feels like socks. Thank you very much, Aunty Joy."

"Well, yes, it is," Aunty Joy would say, looking disappointed. "Aren't you going to open them?"

"All right," Robert would reply, "but it's not so much fun when it's not a surprise."

Now this was hardly fair. No one forced Robert to guess what was in his parcels. It was just a pity he seemed to guess so well. In fact, Robert was very lucky, after a while, that his friends and relations *gave* him presents. It wasn't much fun seeing him open them, after all.

One year, Robert's Uncle Paul

decided to teach him a lesson. He came to visit on Robert's birthday as usual and put a large box on the table in front of his only nephew.

Robert picked up the box. He shook it. He turned it round. He prodded it. He lifted it up and down. He even sniffed at it! He had to confess that he hadn't a clue what was inside.

"Well, open it," said Uncle Paul.

Robert felt rather more interested in this present than in some of the others he had been given. He undid the ribbon and carefully took off the paper. Inside … was another parcel!

"Now you can guess, I expect,"

said Uncle Paul. Once again, Robert
went through his shaking, prodding,
sniffing routine. He still couldn't tell
what was in the parcel.

"So open it," smiled his uncle.

Paul undid the next ribbon.
He took off another layer of wrapping paper to find … yes, you've
guessed, yet *another* colourful
present inside.

"Can't you guess yet?" teased
Uncle Paul.

Robert scowled. He did everything he could think of to the parcel
and wished he had an X-ray
machine. He still couldn't work out
what was inside.

"Open it!" laughed Uncle Paul.

Once again, Robert undid the wrapping paper — only to find another colourful layer inside.

"I don't think there's anything inside here," said Robert. "It's just layer after layer of paper."

"Oh no, it isn't!" said Uncle Paul. "There's quite definitely a present in there, but I'm amazed that you can't work out what it is. You're usually so clever."

That made Robert even more cross. He tore off more and more and more paper, until at last he came to a brightly painted wooden box.

"*Now* what do you think it is?" asked his uncle.

Robert shook the box. There

was no sound. He tapped it. It didn't sound hollow or full, just ordinary. He sniffed it. It didn't smell of anything except wood.

"Well?" asked Uncle Paul. "What is it?"

Robert had to smile. "I don't have a clue," he said. "It's the first present I haven't been able to guess for *ages*." Then he grinned more broadly.

"I suppose," he said, "there is one thing I can say that it definitely *is* … it's a surprise!"

And it was! Turn the page to find out what Robert saw when he opened the box!

Woah! Rocking Horse

What do you do with a rocking horse who is wild? One who bucks and gallops and generally acts as though he is out on the open plains, free to do as he likes? The rocking horse at the Tiny Tots Playgroup was just like that.

In fact, it wasn't really that the rocking horse was nasty and vicious. He didn't mean to send so many little children tumbling from his back when he put on a spurt of speed or kicked up his legs. It was just that the children, very often, were excited to be sitting on the beautiful rocking horse. They grabbed his mane in their plump little hands and kicked their strong little legs into his sides. Well, any horse will get excited as well, if he is treated like that. Sometimes the children shrieked with joy as the horse began to move, and that just made him worse. What with the kicking and the tugging and the shrieking, the rocking horse would leap into action. He would begin to move faster and faster, rearing and rocking higher and higher, until the children screamed with fright

instead of excitement and several of them, as I said before, fell right off on to the carpet.

Luckily, no one was hurt by the wild rocking horse, but most of the children were badly frightened, and they certainly didn't want to sit on the rocking horse again. They didn't understand that if *they* were gentle with the rocking horse, he would be gentle with them.

It was not surprising that the rocking horse soon had a very bad reputation. "Don't go near that horse," the playgroup leader would tell the children. "It's not safe at all."

With no one to ride him, the rocking horse became very sad.

Unfortunately, when a brave child did jump on his back, the rocking horse was so surprised and pleased that he kicked up his heels more than ever. It really was a vicious circle.

Then, one day, a new little girl came to the playgroup. She had

been in hospital for a long time and was still very frail and pale. Although she was nearly four, she couldn't walk very well, and had to be lifted in and out of her chair to sit on the floor at story-time or join the other children singing nursery rhymes.

The little girl did not seem to be interested in anything very much. She had spent so much time by herself that she had forgotten how to play with other children. In any case, she felt so ill and tired a lot of the time that nothing interested her much.

But when the little girl, whose name was Tina, had been at the playgroup for a couple of days, she noticed the rocking horse in the corner.

"I want to ride on *that*," she said. It was the longest sentence that anyone had heard her say.

"I don't think so, Tina," said the playgroup leader. "That horse isn't very safe, and you are not very strong yet. Wait until you are feeling better."

But Tina didn't want to wait. She felt as if she had spent all her life waiting — waiting to go into hospital, waiting for an operation, waiting to feel better, waiting to run around like other children of her age.

Day after day, the little girl made the same request, and at last the playgroup leader agreed. After all, nothing else seemed to interest Tina

The playgroup leader cleared a big space on the floor. She put down a lot of cushions, in case of accidents, and stood nearby to catch the little girl when she fell — as she was sure she would.

But when Tina sat on the horse's back, she didn't pull his mane or kick her feet. She sat quietly and held the reins, feeling the horse beginning to move, ever so slowly.

The playgroup leader was

amazed. Gradually, she began to relax and moved away from the horse, for he was behaving beautifully. No pony ever trotted so gently with a little girl on his back. The horse went slowly, slowly for half an hour, getting to know his rider, until Tina became tired and asked to be lifted down.

After that, Tina rode the big rocking horse every day. And very, very gradually, the horse began to speed up.

As Tina grew stronger, she was able to sit up straighter and hold the reins more tightly. Her eyes began to sparkle and a faint pink colour came to her cheeks. She began to take an interest in other things that were happening at the playgroup, too. Every day she grew happier and healthier.

On the last day of term, Tina's parents came to take her home from playgroup. They were very

pleased with the way she had been improving, but they had never seen her ride the rocking horse, and they did not know why her eyes were brighter and her smiles were broader.

The playgroup leader greeted Tina's parents as they came into the big room. In the corner, a little girl was riding the rocking horse, higher and higher, and faster and faster, her hair flying out behind her as she rode.

"Ah," sighed Tina's mother, "how I hope the day will come when our little girl can do that. It has been such a struggle for her, though she *is* so much better now."

The teacher laughed. "That *is* your little girl," she said "And she's as wild as the rocking horse — I'm very happy to say!"